A Library of Characters

a small collection of big characters

KRITTIKA NIRAULA

TO BABA AND MUMA.
You taught me how to walk and stand on my feet.

AND TO SAMEER.
You give me the wings to fly.

Thank you for your love and support.

PREFACE

I will turn forty this year.
As I sit down to analyze, review, and plan my life
ahead, I asked myself a simple question.

"So, what do I want to do with the rest of my life?"

The answer was simple.

To write and to tell stories.

This book is a small gift from me…to me.
A promise to keep going. A reminder that I am not
yet done, or perhaps I am just getting started.

I hope you enjoy reading my first book.

CONTENTS

INTRODUCTION

Life is a long road, and as a traveler in search of truth, answers, and adventures, we fill our bags with fond memories and great experiences. As we take this fascinating journey through life, we also meet many people along the way. Some make us laugh. Some make us cry. Some hurt us. Some help us. Only a few characters leave a lasting impression, something about their smile, love, even flaws and failings stays back with us, forever.

We do not need an eternity to know someone. Sometimes, a few months, a momentary fling, a quick glance, or even a small, open window to get a glimpse into their world is good enough. The conversations may be incomplete, time may have introduced us only briefly, we may not witness how their stories ended, but we know they were fabulously interesting people. People who are unconventional, open-minded, and ready to embrace life whole-heartedly along with all its mishaps and little messes. This book is about them, inspired by them, and a stroll down old memory lane, remembering them all over again. In this book, I also combine my passion for writing with my love for poetry.

I hope this helps you take a pause and remember all those characters that touched your lives in a special way.

THE MISTER*(Y)* IN BLACK

Even today, the mister wore black shirt, black pants, and sat on the same corner chair. His half-open backpack sat by his feet, all curled up like a lazy cat. As always, he was flipping through a newspaper, with a few more scattered all over the table. *Is he reading the sports section? Is he on the real estate page? Is he married?* His head was down. I was sitting afar. But, even from a distance, I could see his lips move as he read the paper and his eyes smile when he looked around every now and then. Sometimes he also caught me staring at him. His Johnny Depp-like hair, tousled and wild, accentuated his bone structure and hid most of his face. The baby-faced lad was a transparent figure, his personality and innocence shining even under an unkempt, bushy beard.

If his innocence enthralled me, his black clothes enticed me. Black, my favorite, is a tricky color. While it hides our secrets well, the flabs, fears, and insecurities, black also helps our real beauty shine through and come to light. *What was he, the beauty or the beast?* My mind was baffled, and I could not figure him out instantly. So like an obsessed detective at work, I started watching him and his every move for almost six months. He often came to the library, at least four times a week; the mister came early and stayed up until the closing time.

Gradually, I noticed not only he wore black, he wore the same black clothes every time. Meddling in other people's lives is not good, but my curiosity got the best of me. With a microscope in my eyes, I now saw the finer details. His shirt had a few holes, and so did his pants. His black trousers had splotchy brown stains all over; unlike wine, perhaps it was not destined to age gracefully. The zipper of his backpack was broken and the seams ripped open. His black shoes also seemed to have had a rough life. On the surface it was shiny, from behind it was cracked and weathered. The shoe's heels were so thin, his own heels almost touched the ground as he walked. I now knew why he walked with a slight limp. Sometimes, it is soles that reveal a lot about our souls. His soles, now narrated a new story to me. The mister lay exposed to my mind's eyes, as if I could read his private feelings and thoughts, and see everything he has been hiding from the world.

I continued to go to the library, to see him and also in the hope to know him better and deeper. But now, like the rainbow, he showed up only once in a clear blue day. As his visits decreased, a thousand questions pierced my mind, and all kind of emotions ran through my veins. Guilt was eating me up from inside and knocking my conscience's door. *Did he also see me through and found my true intentions? Should I have left him alone? Did I chase him away?*

The detective in me not only failed to solve the case, I lost the case altogether. The mister(y) in black literally evaporated into thin air. Now, an elderly woman sat on his chair. As I walked home, with new books in my hands and the burden of sin on my soul, I could not help but remember a friend. Raymond always said, "Some beauty must be enjoyed and admired only from a distance." Maybe some things, beautiful things, are better left unsolved, unowned, and shrouded in dark veils.

> *There were a million stars*
> *All shining bright*
> *But I chose the one*
> *Whose light was fading*
> *And disappearing.*

YARA: A RARE MOUNTAIN FLOWER

The second floor was the epicenter of this earthquake called Atmos Advertising where ground shook every day. Angry bulls charged and fought with each other for no reason or red flag. Verbal abuses and name-calling rumbled and rattled the entire space as if a storm was on its way. Stale foods, chocolate wrappers, wine bottles, and cigarette stubs further polluted the office atmosphere. Adding to the noise and drama was the printing machine; whole day it whined and howled to the whim of those crazy ad men. The thunder of advertising shook the room, but did not break the spirit of the creative branch that lay sandwiched between client serving and media.

Yara and I walked into this storm. Like me, she was a mountain girl.

Yara, the new bud, was short, petite, and timid. Her white cheeks became the color of ripe tomatoes every time someone talked to her or even uttered her name. A lock of black, silky hair often cascaded down her forehead. She twirled those strands and tucked them behind her ears every time those locks came in her way. Yara hardly wore makeup, tied her hair in a ponytail, wore *salwar kameez* and never left home without a *dupatta* and her Titan watch. Yara was beautiful the old-fashioned way. A teetotaler, Yara did not drink and smoke nor went to clubs and parties. She was a simple, sincere, and contented girl, never expressed the desire to do more with her life.

Both copywriters survived the tempest. Yara and I completed our internships, and now we were out in the real world, giving interviews and looking for our first jobs. We ended up in different companies, and as we became busier with our lives, we drifted apart.

One fine day, Yara called me out of nowhere. It was her birthday, and she wanted to invite me to her party. When I reached Mandarin Oriental, I could not decide if the hotel or my Yara was fancier. Yara stepped out of a cab, sans *dupatta*. She looked so naked. Even her hair was exposed. Brushed and blown, her luscious locks were open and swayed in the wind with uninhibited freedom. A tight dress with a low neckline hugged her body. The only parts covered were her lips and eyes with a bright red lipstick and gold eyeshadow. The bud had blossomed into a flower, but maybe the fragrance, her innocence and vulnerability, was gone.

I met Yara next at a shopping plaza where she invited me home. From a modest girl's hostel, she now lived in a three-bedroom apartment, with her boyfriend. The whole house reeked of Prada, with cigarette smoke hiding behind the strong perfume. Yara showed me around and then disappeared into the kitchen. As I waited in her bedroom, she emerged with two glasses of Margarita rimmed with salt and lime slices. I could not believe it was the same girl who drank only water, not even Coke. As she sat down beside me with her glass, I looked at her face. They say, a beauty of a woman can be seen in her eyes. In her brown eyes, I saw a candle shine bright but slowing losing its glow.

My next meeting with her was at a corporate retreat in Bangalore, an annual convention for copywriters. If Yara's confidence surprised me, her career advancement stunned me. She was now a creative director of a celebrated agency, in just about five years. The young woman, barely 5 feet 2 inches, stood tall on the podium. It was difficult to believe the same girl who could not hold a conversation, today delivered a brilliant presentation leaving the audience awe-inspired. Yara spoke, with perfect diction and rhythm, words cascaded like a waterfall. Her gold Rolex watch sparkled as she moved her neatly manicured red fingers. As I ate my lunch, I glanced over at Yara who was sitting alone staring at her plate. Even in this assembly of people, Yara looked orphaned and away, lost in her own thoughts as if she was in the middle of nowhere or is it lonely at the top?

Yara came in a new machine at Vittorio's Ristorante, on our last meeting. Her bling - a shiny, handsome BMW - looked like a black leopard on the prowl that night. Complementing her car was her new hair, a pixie cut with a side fringe. As we devoured the braised rabbit stew, those locks sat on her forehead, right from starters through desserts, and not once did they seem to bother her! Yara always had a flawless milky complexion, her face so transparent you could almost read her mind. Today she had a cake face; her face slathered with too much foundation and blush. Whether she was trying to hide behind the mask or cover acne scars, I could not tell. All I knew was this new shade was not right for her, or maybe it was just her limelight blinding me.

I saw a change, a metamorphosis, come upon her. I saw the rose become lighter and lighter, its petals withering and falling one by one. Yara's transformation worried me and made me wonder if she finally succumbed to the big, bad world of advertising. For all one knows, changing herself was her only option…the only way for a rose to find a place in this bouquet called life.

My wise sister told me that the name, Yara, also

means butterfly.

> *Maybe I watched a rose wither too soon*
> *Maybe I saw a butterfly come out of her cocoon*
> *It is difficult to see*
> *Which one is she?*

RUN LAATA RUN

"Bhaaga, Laata ayo!"
(Run, Laata is coming!)

A group of girls in school uniforms ran as Laata came after them, limping and dragging his polio-stricken legs. Their skirts flying and shivering in the windy afternoon, like a state flag dancing to the tunes of the national anthem.

Laata was born to run. Laata liked to run. And especially run after girls in skirts.

Everyone was afraid of Laata (a dumb and stupid person in Nepali). Laata was not scared of anyone, except the umbrella. Something about it petrified him. Wise people carried umbrellas, to protect themselves both from rain god's and the beast's wrath.

Laata was omnipresent. He. Just. Was. Everywhere! Laata, like a magician, could pop out from anywhere. From behind the curtains, bushes, alleyways, shops, even under a skirt – he was always at work.

M.G. Marg, Gangtok's downtown, was his hunting ground. The wolf had marked his territory with terror and malice many years ago. A foul smell permeated throughout the plaza, otherwise decked up with roses and orchids in pretty pots. Every other day, a girl was seen running or a group of teenagers beating the beast with umbrellas. Sometimes, even young-looking aunties were not spared, they were chased too.

One day, when Mom and I were strolling and window-shopping, Laata saw me. His brown eyes twinkled. His mouth, salivating at the scent of fresh meat. The fiend, ready to attack. *"Chori, bhaaga,"* my mother warned me in advance. Before the wolf could pounce on me, the brave lioness prepared to fight back. Mom picked up the folds of her sari, tucked them inside her waist, and took out her weapon, a pink umbrella. My mom ran after Laata. Laata ran after me. I just ran, with no plan. The stairs leading down to the supermarket in Lal Bazaar was steep, uneven, and broken in many places. In my heels I scurried away, crushing those little pebbles that blocked my path. Desperately looking for a space to hide and take shelter, I saw a man wave at me, signaling me to come inside. Laata's fear had paralyzed my mind, so much that I hurried into Himalayan Café even at a stranger's invite. Through a broken window in the back of the shop, I could see my mom still running after the madman.

I grew up, from a girl in skirt to a woman in *salwar kameez*. Alongside, the sleepy town burgeoned into a thriving city. Population exploded. New buildings were born. Fancy cars were imported. Tourism skyrocketed. Now, only tourists walked M.G. Marg, locals stopped coming to the crowded plaza. Laata also stopped coming. A newspaper ran a story about a body with deformed legs floating on the Teesta river. Some even say Laata jumped from the Suicide Point, earlier just a deep cliff, now a popular tourist destination. Rumors also say he left Gangtok and went back to his packs, back to the wilderness of Lachung.

Or, maybe Laata is just old and too tired to run.

MARIA GARCÍA

Maria worked hard, even more than the sun. It was six in the morning. Sun was sleeping. Maria was working.

Maria was busy adjusting guides, card inserters, rollers, loading papers, and inspecting her machine. She was using an odd-looking tool for the job. The rest of her gears were carefully tucked inside a big, yellow tool bag that hugged her tiny waist. Christmas was just around the corner, so the entire floor was bedecked in red and white. While life was warm and vibrant here, outside was like a white dream with snow resting upon trees and park benches, and the entire county buried under a snowstorm from the previous night.

Maria was a triple threat: she was the machine operator, the mail examiner, as well as the accountant. The El Salvador *chica* joined Lucas Corporation eons ago, probably when she was 15 or 16 years. Today she is 36. Employees came and left. Bosses resigned. Even machines were replaced every five years. This stubborn girl, glued and fastened to her seat, refused to move.

It is easy to fall in love and stay committed to a fulfilling relationship. There is no reason for a divorce in a happy space. But Maria's job, not only was physically challenging, but also demanding. Like her machine, she worked round the clock. Either Maria had a tremendous tolerance for pain, or she simply enjoyed her work. The warehouse was noisy and dusty, thus adding to the nuisance, but determined and passionate as ever, Maria García stayed married to the job and continued with her responsibilities.

Maria knew everybody. Nobody knew her. Where did she live, what were her hobbies, if she had kids, if she liked dogs, etc., not even the gossipmongers got wind of her life. All we knew was she had a boyfriend back in El Salvador. When I joined the company two months ago, Maria was my trainer. Whatever I know of my job, as a mail examiner, I learned it all from her. On the training ground, the general wanted two things from us: to reach office at seven and work diligently. Maria was a workhorse and had no time to make friends, except for Aldo, Mana, and Mariana, the rest of the world were her acquaintances. Like a chameleon, she changed her colors according to her surroundings. With them, she was like the smiling rainbow. With us, she was black and white - dull, boring, and so mysterious.

During lunch hour every day, as we succumbed to the cold and the dust and the damp of the place, Maria cheerfully waved and signaled the trio to come to the cafeteria. There was a great deal of laughter and congeniality, laced with pranks and jokes that filled the space. Maria was painfully shy, but in their company, she was a total prankster. The four of them looked like a small, happy paradise. The office bathroom was tiny and quaint, and we often heard whispering coming from a corner, a secret meeting run by Maria. No one else was invited, except for her girls. Later, in the evening, as Maria sat down at the entrance to smoke a cigarette, she watched Aldo under the shade of a tree working on his laptop. He was in college, preparing to become a computer technician. She looked at Aldo as if he was her favorite, and her everything.

A few weeks later, our team celebrated Christmas at Tito's Casa, the new Tex-Mex restaurant. It was the 24th of December, and the entire neighborhood was in the spirit of the holidays. I went around to meet everybody; everybody was in the ubiquitous red and white. Aldo looked dashing; he wore a red velvet jacket and black pants, with his hair gelled up and slicked back neatly. I complimented him. He blushed, his color now matching his jacket color. I always wondered about his name; Aldo is a German name, but he looked Hispanic. "Were you named after the famous Aldo brand", I teased him. He smiled. Blushing again, he said, "I was named after my parents, Maria and Naldo." "Even my sisters, Mana and Mariana, were named after them."

As Maria walked passed me, her eyes met mine, and in that brief interaction, I saw her whole life unfold before me, for the first time. Her secrets were now mine.

CHANDRA NIWAS

Chandra Niwas is perched atop a small hillock; a narrow cobblestone road runs to the main entrance of the house. The house consists of two wings – the old and the new. The old is a two floor, wooden, ranch-style built in the 1960s. A double-story house was added later in the 1980s. My grandmother lived in the old wing, my grandfather in the new block.

Houses are like sponges; they gradually imbibe the owner's likes and tastes, even attitudes and feelings. Thus over a period of time, they often become an extension of our own selves. Every nook of the old house reflected my grandmother's tastes and every cranny of the new house bore my grandfather's characteristics.

The old house was torn and tattered, but like a brave soldier, it still had the muscle and the grit to fight many nature's wars. This was the main house, primarily because it had the kitchen and the *puja* room. Grandmother's things – her saris, sweaters, coats, jewelry, knitting yarns and needles scrambled to find space. A glass cabinet, populated with a whole lot of "foreign" items stood in the middle; this was the main attraction of the house. Things granny brought from her England trips or gifts given by her now half-Brit daughter. Like us, local folks who came to meet her were also in awe of those silverwares, lavender mists, potpourri, Scottish bagpipers in skirts, porcelain plates, and dolls. Those dolls always wore gorgeous attires, all thanks to my granny's great fashion sense and knitting skills. Black and white family photos adorned the walls, along with a wooden clock that rang every hour.

Like a loyal bodyguard, the new house - my grandfather's station - stood next to the old house. Newspapers, men's clothes, telescope, army trunks, world maps, globes, and stacks of books occupied the first floor. Filled with sitars, violins, harmoniums and an abundance of peace and light, the second floor was an ideal musical retreat. With a terrace built on top, house members had free access to the lovely view of the village and the valley. The sunrise was a bonus. A row of roses, marigolds, and orchids covered the verandah area, with a couple of hanging plants in the front and a big tree in the back. Doors and windows of both houses were always open for fresh air, warm sun, street dogs, friends, and guests.

Every year, my family along with aunts and uncles on my father's side visited Takdah. We went to the quaint Himalayan village to celebrate *Dashain* (Dusshera festival) with my grandparents. *Dashain* was a breather in my life, like a picnic break from the rut and routine of my school life. Perhaps, it was a welcome change for the house too; from two, now an army of people (and their dogs) came to live under its roof.

A state of utter chaos, confusion, and clutter, such was life for the rest of the stay. Because my grandparents stayed alone and also had two houses to maintain, thus things were a bit messy and disorganized. Working out sleeping arrangements was difficult. Things worked on a first come, first serve basis, and early birds always took the best bedrooms. The rest looked like a close-knit unit as they slept on the floors huddled together trying to find space and keep warm. Bath time was rough; there was no comfort of a hot bath. Mealtime was tumultuous but fun. When organic vegetables, *desi gheu* (ghee), wood fire, and my mom's hands worked together, the dinner plate was pure magic. The fire from the *mato ko chulha* (mud stove) also kept the house warm. Afternoons in Takdah are sunny, but evenings and nights, especially in the *Dashain* month of October can get really cold. An *angithi* (mud heater) also provided extra heat; drinking *chiya* (tea) and eating *murai* (rice puffs) around the fire was an event for a city girl like me. A *jharna* (stream of water) just behind the kitchen provided water for drinking and cleaning. Playtime was unique. With no toys in the house, children settled with stones, shells, told stories to each other, enjoyed the sweeping vistas from the terrace and occasionally went for walks. They also played a game of dice in the *bazaar* (market) and in the house, at night.

Night was colorful, noisy, and truly sinful at Chandra Niwas. Children and adults played cards all night long, mostly rummy and flash. Folks, like my uncle, always got rich and few wallets, like mine, were always empty at the end. *Raksi* (alcohol) and *pakku* (a mutton specialty) was a part of the package, and the generous adults even allowed the kiddos to take a sip or two of those wines and vodkas. After a few hours of merriment, eyes reddened, mouths stammered, and people argued and tripped over each other. Inside, the climate was hot and intense. Outside, the night air was cool and crisp, with nature showcasing a Beethoven-like performance. Croaking frogs, buzzing fireflies, chirping crickets, and howling foxes provided a perfect background score to children's performance on the verandah. We, children, sang and danced, and watched the sky. The night sky was beautiful – a big moon and a million stars always smiled upon us.

After *Dashain* was over, people packed their belongings and kids, and left, one family at a time.

The spare mattresses and blankets went back to their secret caves. Bedsheets and pillow covers hung up to dry in the sun. Extra plates and utensils, carefully tucked away in the storeroom. The kitchen and the entire house now moped for a final time. Group photos clicked for one last time. Hugs and kisses exchanged, and the vacation ended with promises to return to Takdah next year. *Oh! dear, hellos are sweet, goodbyes, always bitter!*

Promises were kept, and the following year we all met again and continued the merrymaking with more *rakshi* and *pakku*. This tradition, of going to Takdah to celebrate *Dashain*, continued for about 30 years. Even after Grandfather expired, we kept going to the house for Grandmother up until 2011. She expired in 2016.

Chandra was the name of my grandmother's mother. Niwas means a house where a family lives together. Today, Chandra Niwas is empty, with its kith and kin tucked away in various corners of the world and busy with their own lives. People may have gone, but a few things stayed back. The sounds of laughter are forever trapped within its walls and so is granny's perfume; it still lingers on her sweaters and coats. Those dolls might have a missing arm or an eye, but they still wear the same knitted sweaters. Those wooden floorboards, wrinkled and squeaky, still have faint traces of footprints, probably hiding in shame. The wall clock may not chime every hour, but it tells time. The brown *rarri* (woolen blanket) on which we sat, year after year, for *tika* ceremony on tenth day of *Dusshera* might have a few holes, but it will keep you warm.

As for the two peas in a pod, Grandpa and Grandma, they continue to live…in my heart, in my memory, and in my stories.

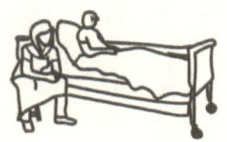

THE DYING MAN

Man smiled at Life
Man gave his heart, held its hands
Life became his best friend
But when Man was in pain
Life chose to have him slain
Man's smile was broad till the end
Even in his goodbye, Man said hello my friend!

Love is celebrated. Death is mourned. Love is a language we are taught from the moment we are born. Death is a subject that does not make it to our textbooks or dining table conversations. Parents often find the need, almost like an impulse, to protect their children, not just from sickness, but also from the concept of death. Because we are kept away from the truth, misconceptions, fears, even its mere existence, when death comes to take people we love, we are at a loss. While we grieve, we become so busy – denying, praying, talking to doctors and friends, and coping with the news, that we forget death is about them, not us. It is about the person dying. It is about how they are dealing and what they are feeling.

Jeevan, my friend, was a dying man. At the cruel age of 41, he was diagnosed with advanced liver cancer, and after various tests and careful analysis, doctors declared he would live only for a few more months. When I went to meet him, Jeevan was sleeping in his hospital bed with tapes and bandages and needles poked in his pale hands. Fluids from two plastic bags flowed through a tube into his body; the nurse said one was his food, other, his water. Jeevan in his mechanical cot, attached with drips, oxygen tanks, and heart monitors looked like a rat in a lab. A nightstand had an old clock that did not tell time, fresh flowers dying in a vase, and tons of medicines strips scattered all over. Only from the look of his new bedroom, Jeevan looked like a dying man. Otherwise, like his name, Jeevan was alive and kicking, with a desire to live. So much was the yearning and the will, the dying man told me he wanted to be reborn tomorrow if he died today.

Painkillers and anesthesia only numbed his pain, not his feelings and desires. Jeevan wanted to continue living, and enjoy the little joys and surprises of life. Instead of, "How is your pain?" Jeevan wanted to hear "Are you happy?" from people who visited him. A white dove came by, every afternoon. The bird tucked into the shade of the windowsill and drank water from a ceramic ashtray that Jeevan had converted into a birdbath. My friend looked forward to his friend's visit. I do not know how he could wait, wait so patiently for hours just for a glimpse of that little guy. Waiting is hard, but perhaps, waiting was all he had, for now, and ever. Jeevan often said, "When your stay becomes long, people's visit becomes short." Earlier people used to show up with flowers, fruits, chocolates, Bournvita and Marie biscuits, now only a little bird and I came to see him. Jeevan wished how he could get his phone back, to take a picture of the dove. Because his wife thought his iPhone might get lost or stolen in the chaos of this unfamiliar terrain, she took his cell phone home and locked it up in her cupboard. "Isn't it strange to switch off a living man's cellphone?" he smirked and told me once.

The dying man enjoyed many things, but nothing came close to the early morning that stretched out before him, like the arms of a kind woman. As he crawled out of his warm bed and stood barefoot on the cold balcony, Jeevan smiled and said hello to the world. Jeevan was not sure if he still belonged, to anyone. He wished his wife could join him: to see the first light of the day, to hear the rustling of leaves, to taste the air, to soak in the silence. Avantika was a good person; she came to see him, occasionally brought flowers, visited temples and prayed hard, but in the grieving process, she forgot that Jeevan was also a husband and not just a patient, not just a dying man. In the quiet loneliness of dawn, he often wrote her name in his foggy bedroom window. Jeevan really missed his wife, in the little things.

Jeevan often walked down the nostalgia path, not just to cope with his death, but also to live life all over again. He never got tired of talking how much he danced at his wedding or how happy he was when his son was born. Jeevan also went further back, to his school and college, and retold dirty little jokes from those days. He kept a photo album in his drawer, hidden away from his wife. She thought it was bad for his eyes. She did not know it was good for his heart. Jeevan loved to go through old photographs and tell the full story behind each photo, narrating events and remembering even the minute details as if it all happened yesterday.

Jeevan loved his past, but wanted to live in the present, and most important, live a normal life. He wanted to experience everything that was happening to him and around him, without missing any rhythm and beat. People could not see him beyond cancer and his failing body; they could not see the little wants and wishes of a man. On several occasions, I saw Jeevan beg his wife to get him a cigarette. Not that he was getting withdrawal symptoms and badly wanted to smoke. All he wanted to do was to take a deep drag, and feel the smoke go in and fill his lungs. Jeevan also missed being in the family frame, gardening with his wife, playing soccer with his son, going for walks with his dog, painting in his attic. Of all things, he missed the smell of freshly baked cookies running throughout his house every Sunday morning. As days passed by, Avantika came less frequently and neither brought Rohan, their son. Jeevan taught or perhaps tricked his heart into believing that she was busy running the show in his absence. A small part of Avantika still hoped his death was a dream or a hoax, but she was not oblivion to the unpleasant reality either. Keeping busy was the only way she knew to cope with what was happening around. The mother in her was also in a dilemma, she thought lying to her son or not bringing him to the hospital was the only way to protect Rohan. Avantika was worried how the little one would respond to the truth about his father.

Jeevan was not ready for a departure, not so soon, not just yet. Cancer was not killing him; world's pity and the constant reminder of his end was stabbing him multiple times, each day, each minute. He wanted his death to be a beautiful experience, but alas, we turned it into an ugly spectacle and made it all about us.

PUPPY LOVE

My previous relationship did not last long, but it still impacts me to the point that it haunts me sometimes. He left a bittersweet taste in my mouth, the way strong coffee leaves a lingering aftertaste. The separation was not dramatic; it was sudden and excruciating. When we separated, we gave each other a painful parting gift. I gave him a feeling of being unloved, rejected, and abandoned. He gave me the gift of not knowing.

And this - not knowing - can be the worst feeling in the world.

I still do not know what happened to him.

The puppy was a bony little thing, with bones sticking out from all quarters of his debilitated body. Sad but hopeful, his eyes could melt anyone's heart. A brown kombai, about four months old, the little bundle of energy had pendant ears, a black wet nose, and a humble name. His name was Puppy.

Alpha Dog House, a renowned non-profit in Bangalore, rescued street and injured dogs, but once they brought them in, Alpha ignored the hapless beings. Mealtime was, once a day. Bath time was, once a month. Playtime was, rare. Love given, none. Being an animal lover and an affable person, I make friends easily. I could not in Alpha, neither with any human nor with any dog. The doctors and administrative staff spoke only Kannada, very little English and no Hindi. If the language barrier restricted me, the mongrels' temperament (and condition) scared me. Those dogs, bound to the walls with heavy chains, looked ferocious. Also, the sight of any human made them more irate. Maybe we reminded them of their street days and those kicks and stones flung at them. I was the new veterinarian, and perhaps the only person who genuinely loved animals.

Puppy was the warmth in that cold place.

I was in love with Puppy right from the start. He took time to respond and reciprocate my love, but gradually the puppy trusted me and recognized that my feelings were genuine. We also had a thing or two in common; he hated the place like me, and I was scared of the other dogs like him. Soon we were the new lovers in town, totally inseparable, always stuck to each other; *what to do, love is like glue!* Whenever he saw me, Puppy squealed, swung his tail like a pendulum, jumped up and down, and scratched the rails of his cage. And when I slipped my arms through those rails, he licked my fingers as though they were coated with sugar crystals. Sometimes, during my lunch breaks, we went for walks and played with Frisbee at the park. Puppy often came to my lap, played with my scarf or hair while watching me with his hypnotic brown eyes.

A month later, when Puppy was five months old, Alpha people started discussing him. Puppy was just another case, an unnecessary burden to them. The shelter could not continue looking after him, probably due to budget constraints or they thought Puppy was not safe in that place. Being the only puppy in the shelter, he was often teased, nagged, and subjected to abuses by dogs, bigger and powerful than him, angrier than him. The shelter was desperately looking to either dispose or relocate him. The man who brought the sick puppy was untraceable. Other rescue houses were full. No one wanted to adopt him. Euthanasia, the painful option, was also being considered.

I still remember vividly that it was the spring of the year 2004. My darling was sitting quietly in his coop. When he saw me, his eyes smiled, and he danced around wagging his tiny tail, so surprised, so excited as though he was seeing me for the first time. Poor thing did not know he was seeing me for the last time. I had resigned, and tomorrow I was flying back to my homeland, Gangtok.

That evening, as I packed my bags, tears would not stop flowing, a myriad of emotions disturbed me, and guilt poisoned my mind. Another worst feeling is feeling unloved, rejected, and most of all, abandoned. And I was giving all of it to somebody.

The next day as I waited in the crowded terminal to board my flight, Puppy was there in his room, waiting for me...waiting for the only person who cared about him.

In this sea of people
Why am I drowning
Alas! no one is coming to save me
For my savior is far away...
...drowning in his own sea of misery.

MR. AND MRS. RANA

There is something about the mountain air. Not only does it smells fresh, but sweet too. The air became cleaner and crisper as we approached a hairpin bend, at Batasia Loop. As my driver steered his way on its meandering curve, colorful houses clustered together on the hilly slope welcomed me. They looked like matchboxes stacked on top of each other. Surrounding those little dwellings were straight pine trees that looked no less than soldiers in uniform silently protecting the hills. The whistling of the toy train, the chuffing and puffing of the classic steam engine, echoed through the valley as my jeep moved. Finally, when I saw the snow-capped, glistening peaks of Kanchenjunga poised against a clear blue sky, my heart stopped beating. I knew I was home.

I was twenty-three and starting my first job as a veterinary doctor, in Darjeeling. It was Friday and I had to join my clinic on Monday. With less than three days to find a place to stay, I went around town frantically looking for an accommodation. As luck would have it, all the women's hostels were full, now Rana's Abode was my only shred of hope. Rana's Abode, turned out to be a men's hostel. I could not believe I was alone and homeless here, even in my place of birth. Whether it was my tired legs or my despondent soul, something inside me broke. In the most unlady-like fashion, I dropped my suitcases down on the carpeted floor, plunked down on their couch, and started crying. Looking at my alarming state, Mrs. Rana held my hands and calmed me, "You can use our daughter's bedroom," she said. Their daughter was in college, in Delhi, and she was not coming back anytime soon. I became a part of their family and started living with Mr. and Mrs. Rana.

Most relationships rust with time. Even the happiest couples crumble under the weight and pressure of the rock that marriage is. Mr. and Mrs. Rana survived the test of time because even after nearly twenty-five years, the knot was tight, the vows remembered, and their love, fresh and invigorating as the Darjeeling air.

If love kept them together, tennis brought the lovebirds even closer. Martina Hingis was Mrs. Rana's favorite. Mr. Rana admired Roger Federer. Regardless of the different tastes and opinions, the couple enjoyed the French Open and other joys of life with unrivaled passion; they were united even when they were divided. Apart from watching sports, cooking was another of the couple's favorite pastime. The wife loved to watch her husband work his magic in the kitchen, with her secret recipes. Both enjoyed reading newspapers and solving crosswords. Not only they completed their puzzles together, but also finished each other's sentences. Every evening they went for a rejuvenating stroll in the tea garden. Each morning the couple sat on the balcony with their piping cups of tea, to watch the sunrise. When the orange halo emerged from behind the mountaintop, the pair looked into each other's eyes and welcomed it with a kiss. Something about the sun moved them. Perhaps sunrise gave them the strength to keep going. Perhaps the possibility of a new day instilled hope in their hearts, a feeling that their relationship will survive anything life throws at them.

The day we celebrated their 25th wedding anniversary was my last day with Mr. and Mrs. Rana.

Days turned into weeks. Spring into winter. Just like seasons, my life was about to change. I was getting married in three months. As I prepared my guest list, Mr. and Mrs. Rana came to my mind; the two of them in a frame looked so beautiful, so perfect. There was no communication with them for over eight years, but their memories and generosity stayed with me. I could never forget how they had opened their doors and hearts for me when no one else did.

On my wedding day, as I stood on the stage with folded hands and a smile, my eyes wandered towards the doorway. A pot-bellied man in a gray suit and blue tie walked in, a rose bouquet covering his face. When he came close, I saw his face, but could not recognize the man standing before me. Some men get better with age. Mr. Rana did not. Somewhere between the wrinkles, white hairs, and the receding hairline, I was trying to find the person I once knew, a charming, handsome man with a wild laugh and vivacious energy.

"*Namaste*, Mr. Rana, thank you so much for coming."

"Hello *chori*, congratulations."

"Thanks. How have you been?"

"Well...doing good."

"Where is Mrs. Rana?"

"She's somewhere...busy...you know."

That short conversation conveyed a lot. His sad eyes said it all. My father told me later that Mr. and Mrs. Rana separated, shortly after I left their place.

Here I was as a newlywed, looking forward to a new beginning and hoping my relationship would be like theirs, in amity and forever together. Mr. and Mrs. Rana, to me, was a couple whose marriage was made in heaven. As congratulatory messages kept raining down on me and the jubilant atmosphere reverberated with happy music, I wept bitterly inside.

Unable to accept this new reality, my restless mind revisited their house, the nest by the tea garden, the beautiful life they had built for themselves. I found myself retaliating and fighting my emotions, even doubting all that I saw with my own eyes when I stayed with them. Why did I not notice the cracks in their relationship? How could their love have blinded me so much that I could not see the truth staring at my face?

Probably time changes everything. Probably some happy beginnings have sad endings.

We built a house, brick by brick
We put a roof over our worries
A pillar to support our dreams
A floor to roll out our fantasies
One day a storm knocked our door
Alas! we opened that door!

ICE MAIDEN

Ice Maiden, in a blue chiffon sari and white heels, looked like a model straight out of Vogue magazine as she walked her black Labrador. Like a high fashion model, she wore a straight, sullen face, as if she was angry at life. She rarely smiled or said hello to people. After the stroll, she left her dog tied to a bench in front of the staffroom. The beast sat on the floor all day without whining or making a sound. Her students also behaved pretty much the same way. A firm and strict disciplinarian, her students never had lively discussions, free exchange of thoughts, or any classroom entertainment. A living organism, immobilized and frozen, my new history teacher was cold and full of mystery. My classmates thought the moniker, Ice Maiden, will be a perfect fit.

A tall, slim, spectacled woman in her late 30s, Mrs. Malati Pradhan, had a soft face and a peach complexion. However, it was her eyes that had caught my attention right from the first day. A beautiful hazel colored, and as much as they enhanced her beauty, whenever I looked at them, all I saw was infinite sadness. As if a heart was broken inside and the pieces still hurt her. Through the noise and the chaos and the crowd of the classroom, her eyes often communicated to me, as if she was trying to tell me something important. During one of our American history classes, she opened a chapter on Titanic's maiden voyage and the sea disaster that followed. When she explained how the massive ship hit an iceberg, ruptured its hull, and sank, I thought Mrs. Pradhan, through this great story, was trying to narrate her story, to me.

By the end of the second semester, her doleful eyes had consumed me. Slowly I started seeing dark spots in her white light. Mrs. Pradhan often wore jarring makeup, and I always wondered the need to touch up when her real beauty was enough. Soon I discovered why. Once when she came to take the last class of the day, like our energy, even her makeup was starting to wear off. That is when I saw a stitch scar on her left cheeks camouflaged by a heavy foundation, along with a deep cut on her lips, which otherwise remained underneath a dark lipstick.

Desperate to see more, the real face behind the mask, my eyes searched every corner of her body as she talked and moved, in the classroom and outside. I do not know why was I so fascinated by her wounds, after all, even the beautiful moon has blacks spots. My foolish and clouded mind somehow was unable to accept beauty in any other form.

Mrs. Pradhan always left her hair open, even on hot summer days. But once, on Teacher's Day, when the whole school was dressed up in florals and ribbons, Mrs. Pradhan turned up in a magenta silk sari; she looked stunning, and so did her hair. Her wild locks were tamed in a tight bun, with a red rose carefully tucked in. The bun was low, and so was her blouse. The intricate *zardozi* work on her blouse enticed me. As I got busy admiring the exquisite craftsmanship, some ugly lines on the beautiful space traumatized my eyes. There were a couple of angry red lines that ran all across her back as if someone was whipping her with a firm fist. At home, there was someone who had drawn a line that she could not cross. I wanted to touch her scars and feel the pain. The teachers sat on a raised platform for the felicitation ceremony; it was bright and lit by spotlights. As sweat trickled down her rosy cheeks, it stopped for a moment on a deep cleft hidden by her eyebrow. I could not immerse myself in the celebration anymore, it was seriously getting difficult to sit back and just enjoy the show.

The helpless girl in me kept staring at her pain.

My 8th grader mind could read the hidden messages, but could not fully understand the gravity of the situation or gather the courage to speak to someone. I had no choice but to trick myself into believing that Mrs. Pradhan was born with those scars and marks, that she was all right. I kept quiet for the rest of the year. She stayed quiet too.

Now that I am through school and college, and have matured too, I can read those signs and decipher their meanings with better clarity. I finally understand that when a scar begins to tell its story, it is not always a sad narrative. I also understand that life is not fair and maybe Mrs. Pradhan had to engage in a few personal battles. Maybe she fought with all her might and solemnity, and back then when our paths crossed, she was just recovering and healing from her wounds. Ice is cold, but ice is also used for preservation. Maybe her frozen exterior, her silence was to preserve her dignity, pride, and self-respect. Perhaps, Ice Maiden was Iron Maiden, and those mystery marks were scars of grit and resilience, her weapons that she may have adopted to persevere or survive pain and abuse for years, even decades.

BON VOYAGE, PAPA!

In loving memory of my father-in-law
(1943 – 2012)

A tall, moist, multi-layered chocolate cake, slathered with heaps of a decadent vanilla frosting. This is what comes to my mind when I think of my father-in-law. A life rich in experiences. A life of high adventures. A life filled with delicious moments. Papa had a voracious appetite for life and he was hungry till the end. Very few people recognize the need, purpose, and meaning of life. Papa was a wise man. Not only he saw life as life, but also as an opportunity to make it large and to joyfully celebrate it. Full, well-nourished, and satiated with pleasure; such was Papa's heart when he went away for his final rest.

My first recollection of Papa is that of a man at Mumbai airport. A big, milky-white person, in his usual black pants and white shirt, waddling from side and side and waiting for us at the international terminal. Because we live away from the homeland, we miss the love and warmth of family so much. It was comforting seeing him at the airport, his presence was like a reassuring squeeze of the hand. He always came no matter what; it was probably his way to let us know we are not alone, that we have a family waiting for us back home. Our India trips always started and ended with my father-in-law.

For many, nothing feels better than the idea of going home to loved ones, eating home-cooked meals, watching TV and spending time with children. Papa was also a family man, but not in the traditional sense. My father-in-law had the spirit of a traveler, the soul of an adventurer, and a heart full of desire to travel and explore the world; the world was both his oyster and home. So, early on in his life, Papa made a choice from his heart to walk an unconventional path and create a little life for himself while still performing his duty as a husband and father. When Papa was all of 32, my husband was born and when his youngest son was barely three months old, the traveler took his first big step forward. America was his maiden foreign trip, and after that, there was no looking back – at his old life. The adventurer kept going out in the world, striking cities off his bucket list, adding more pins on his map, and decorating his passports with colorful stamps. The maverick that he was, Papa even converted my marriage into a road trip. It is seriously difficult to believe even now that he drove all the way from Mumbai to Gangtok, a distance of about 1500 miles. When he arrived at my wedding, with his gang of friends, little did we know he had come in his Mahindra Bolero! The traveler came, blessed us, and disappeared again, just after two days. Someone later informed us that Papa was planning a trip to Kolkata. This is how he was, no one knew about his trips, not even his family. Even when he visited us, our house was just a stopover for him. The first time he came to meet us, in 2010, he stopped in Dallas en route to Alaska. The second time, the last trip of his life, was a stopover from Chile.

Papa's desire and drive to travel was so strong that even when his health failed him and doctors tried to scare him, he would rightfully get back at them. One time, he got a paralytic attack on his way to the airport to catch a flight to Russia. The flight left without him and back at the hospital doctors declared he may never walk again. Papa, as stubborn as he was, not only made sure he sprinted, but also traveled to Russia to see what he missed the first time. Now that I look back, it seems Russia and Papa loved playing hide-and-seek with each other. When my father-in-law was diagnosed with cancer in early 2012, his doctors informed us that he had only a few months to live. Papa had booked his Moscow flight, probably his third visit, just before this premonition. But, he kept holding on to his plane ticket even though his condition was deteriorating day by day. Perhaps that ticket gave him the hope and courage to keep fighting, or he thought he could win this time too.

Papa believed in traveling light, and all he ever carried was a small suitcase with a few clothes and a brown, woolen blanket, even to summer destinations. Because Papa was a solo-traveler, maybe his blanket reminded him of home or was like a friend to him. The traveler never brought back photographs to flaunt, magnets for his fridge, or any kind of mementos from his trips. *His walls never got to dress up; they were always minimum, and so bare.* The voyager brought home only one gift, tons of stories for his family and friends.

Papa also believed in traveling light through the journey of life. A generous person, his heart was enormous and always open; Papa had space and strength and the will to accommodate the world. Being a successful builder in Mumbai, my father-in-law could have easily created a goldmine for him and his family. But the kind of person he was, Papa made sure everyone around him, and not just his wife and sons, were happy, comfortable, and rich enough. He purchased apartments for his loved ones. Each time he upgraded his vehicle, he would give away his old car to a cousin or friend. He offered to take care of parties, vacations, and other events. For my own wedding, Papa sent invitation cards to his extended family, friends and their friends, along with flight tickets. The magnanimous person he was, Papa took care of people falling behind on their bills, even big loans. My father-in-law never got tired; he kept giving right till the end.

One fine morning, Papa picked up his suitcase along with his blanket and said, *"Main hospital ja raha hoon, ek ya do dino main vaapas aa jaoonga. Chinta mat karo, sab theek ho jayega"* (I am going to the hospital and will be back in one or two days. Don't worry, everything will be all right). These were his last words to me. We lost him the next day; he ended his journey here to begin a new one somewhere else. The traveler went away for his final journey, wrapped up in his favorite blanket.

A father often leaves his son a house and all the money he can earn and save in his lifetime. Papa was different. He left behind a great legacy of goodwill and generosity with which he lived, and it still lives on in the hearts of the people he touched. The traveler left his most prized possession for my husband and me. A bag full of passports soaked with his memories, fingerprints, and footprints of more than fifty countries. Papa showed us the road on which we now travel and continue the journey he started. Not only the joy of traveling, Papa also showed us the beauty of giving.

A traveler never stops
A journey never ends
Only destinations change
Desires still the same
Keep giving, keep going
May the adventures continue
Your footprints run through
Across new peaks and untrodden avenues.
Bon voyage, Papa!

AUTHOR'S NOTE

I consider *A Library of Characters* as a work of life. These characters were marooned in the past, and it had been a while since I visited them. Recreated from memories, I have tried to remain as faithful to my encounters and experiences with them. I may have fictionalized the characters' names, locations, and a few other things, but my interactions with them are real. My feelings are genuine.

I would like to thank Sudipta Bhattacharya for his support, encouragement, and generosity. He took the time out from his busy schedule to read my drafts, offer precise suggestions, and helped me see my own writing in a new light. I also learned a lot through our interactions, especially how important it is to make time for others.

Finally, many thanks to my husband, Sameer. His feedback, both positive and negative, was a precious gift throughout the process of writing this book.

ABOUT THE AUTHOR

 Krittika Niraula was born in Darjeeling and raised in Gangtok. A mountain girl to the core, she finds big joys in little things, likes to go for long walks and disappear into the wilderness. In a former life, she was a veterinary doctor and a copywriter. An avid dog lover, she now works as a writing tutor and also helps local clients with their content needs. She regularly writes on her blog (iamviwa.com), her favorite place to publish her work including poems. She often returns to her childhood, home, and hometown, to reconnect with the past. Nostalgia is her favorite pastime, an indulgence, and a source of many of her stories. An observer of the world and a restless soul, this book is a collage of some of those observations.

Krittika lives in Dallas with her husband.